With My
Rifle
by My Side

A Second Amendment Lesson

Other books by **Kimberly Jo Simac**

American Soldier Proud and Free
Illustrated by Donna Goeddaeus

***When I Grow Up
I'm Going to Be a Hockey Star***

Girls Play Hockey too!

With My
Rifle
by My Side

A Second Amendment Lesson

Written by
Kimberly Jo Simac

Illustrated by
Donna Goeddaeus

With My Rifle by My Side
A Second Amendment Lesson

by Kimberly Jo Simac

Illustrated by Donna Goeddaeus

Copyright © 2010 by Kimberly Jo Simac

International Standard Book Number: 978-0-9827074-4-9

Library of Congress Control Number: 2010929321

Editor: Emily Kirk Phillips

Managing Editor & Production:
Desta Garrett

Printed in the United States of America
by Jostens Press

Young Heart Books
Nordskog Publishing Inc.

Nordskog Publishing, Inc.
2716 Sailor Avenue
Ventura, California 93001, USA
1-805-642-2070 • 1-805-276-5129

www.NordskogPublishing.com

MEMBER
CSPA
CHRISTIAN SMALL PUBLISHERS ASSOCIATION

To all who believe

in freedom.

Introduction

The "Right to Bear Arms" is a Constitutional right embodied in the Second Amendment. It is a fundamental link to the heritage left to us by our nation's Founders. *With My Rifle by My Side* is a story that conveys this right to children and teaches the honor and responsibility that come with the ownership and handling of guns.

If America is to persist, we must stop indoctrination so contrary to the beliefs passed down to us. It is our duty and responsibility to defend the ideals and principles that our Constitution was founded upon and restore the link to our heritage.

It is time for Americans to stand up and defend the country that has offered so much to its citizens. For too long we have reaped the bountiful harvest America offers and not sown a single seed. The result is a transformation of America that has rendered *Lady Liberty* helpless to defend and protect her people.

The Founders predicted such demise if we strayed from the fundamental premise that government should serve the people and not the reverse. Because we have lost sight of our original values, now our morals, work ethic, pride, and integrity have been greatly diminished.

How will American children realize their ability to achieve greatness if no one instills such attributes as courage, integrity, and honesty in their hearts and minds? We must dedicate ourselves to equipping our children with the tools they need so that they may carry on the rich heritage of America. We must teach our children at an early age that our rights and freedoms as Americans are fragile and of utmost importance. And we can impart a love for liberty, which we have inherited because of our Founders' understanding of righteousness and justice. Only then will they be able to achieve greatness and preserve the great legacy of America.

With My Rifle by My Side is a book that works to instill such values and principles in children. It is a unique story that celebrates duty, honor, and liberty at a time when such ideals are being banned and assaulted in our schools and general society. This book will inspire children to take their place as the future leaders of our nation.

– Kimberly Jo Simac

When summer is over

and the school year is here,
I know that it's close
    to my favorite time of year.

The days all get shorter;
the leaves all turn brown.

We watch the geese fly above
and travel to warmer ground.

We love to go out
   with our Dad in the truck.
He loads corn and apples
   for the does and the bucks.

We drive to the fields
    to bait Dad's hunting stands.
We know we are blessed
    to hunt on this land.

I like to use my rifle,
   but shooting is not play.
Dad teaches me safety;
   we review the rules each day.

We set up the targets
   on big bales of hay.
Before we start practice,
   Dad shows me the right way.

To handle a rifle requires
caution and care.
I listen to Dad and respect
all that he shares.

We traveled to our capital,
Washington, D.C.,
to learn all about
our nation's history.

We heard the great stories
of brave men from the past,
who wrote the best rules
to make America last.

The Founding Fathers trusted God
for the rules they would make.
They warned us of decisions
that could lead us all astray.

They said it's our privilege,
responsibility, and right,
to own our own guns,
and be ready to fight.

With their rifles by their sides,
  they protected their right to be free.
They defended their land, neighbors,
  towns, and families.

We also learned of heroes
  who gave their lives to make us free.
It was then I started to realize,
  just what America means to me.

Back at home, we have our supper,
and we bow our heads to pray.
Dad thanks God for our food
and the gift of every day.

We pray for an America
    that is safe and strong in heart.
And I know as I grow older,
    I will learn to do my part.

With respect and safety,
  I'll keep my rifle by my side.
I will honor and remember
  all those who fought and died.

I will always love America;
  it is a part of me.
And I will always be prepared
  to protect my family.

The
End

Appendix for Parents and Grandparents

includes

Gun Safety for Children

The Second Amendment

A Word from the Publisher

About the Author & About the Illustrator

Safety First!

While discussing firearms, safety must be taught first and foremost. Even if guns are not accessible in your home, young children need to know what to do if they ever do come across a gun without you there. The youngest of children must be taught that guns are dangerous, and that they should never touch them without your permission and close guidance. Listed below are some general safety rules for the handling of firearms. Please consult your firearm manufacturer, or other reliable source for precise safety rules and maintenance of your firearms.

Safety and respect for rifles and guns

- A child should never touch or handle a rifle or gun without adult supervision.

- A child must always listen to their adult supervisor and respect the rules.

- Always be aware of where your rifle or gun is pointed.

- Always treat your rifle or gun as if it is loaded.

- Take great care how you hold a rifle or gun while at ease or walking.

- You must learn how to operate a rifle or gun correctly and practice shooting at targets for precision.

- You must never have your finger on the trigger when not aiming to shoot. Pressing the trigger of your rifle or gun will fire its bullets.

- When not being used, a rifle or gun should be unloaded of bullets, and stored in a safe and securely locked case.

- A child must never touch or handle a rifle or gun without adult permission and supervision.

– Compiled by Kimberly Jo Simac and Tom Maillette

Links to Gun Organizations and Programs

Gun Owners of America—GOA
Larry Pratt, *Executive Director*

http://gunowners.org

> GOA's mission is to preserve our Second Amendment rights. To learn more, please visit their Website.

The National Rifle Association—NRA
Ronald L. Schmeits, *President*; Wayne LaPierre, *Vice President*

www.home.nra.org/#/home

"NRA Programs"
   http://www.nra.org/programs.aspx

"Education & Training"
   http://www.nrahq.org/education/index.asp
   "NRA Gun Safety Rules"
   http://www.nrahq.org/education/guide.asp

"Eddie Eagle Information for Parents"
   http://www.nrahq.org/safety/eddie/infoparents.asp

Boy Scouts of America—BSA
www.scouting.org

> For families who are interested, the Boy Scouts of America offers shooting activities at instructional camps for Cub Scouts (approximately ages 7 to 10) that include archery and BB guns but not firearms.

> For Boy Scouts (approximately 11 and up), additional shooting activities are offered, under similar circumstances, but activities can also include shotguns, muzzle loaders and rifles.

> For information on Cub Scout and Boy Scout shooting activities, visit their "Guide to Safe Scouting: Guns and Firearms" page: www.scouting.org/scoutsource/healthandsafety/gss/gss08.aspx

The Second Amendment
of the Constitution of the United States of America reads:

"A well regulated militia, being necessary to the security of a free state, the right of the people to keep and bear arms shall not be infringed."

The Second Amendment for Children, and Their Parents and Grandparents:

With My Rifle by My Side talks about having a rifle to protect our liberty and to protect our families. Because liberty was so important to the Founders of the United States of America, they wanted to be sure that the people of the States would be able to fight for their freedom. Even though war and fighting are very serious, and are things we should never take lightly, we need to know that sometimes they are needed to defend our rights or our families. Owning and using a gun is a serious responsibility and privilege, and American citizens should be allowed to own and use guns to protect themselves. The Founders knew how important it is to protect our liberty and to protect our families, so they wrote the Second Amendment to make sure the government wouldn't try to take guns away from the people.

Our Founders stated:

"No Free man shall ever be debarred the use of arms." (Thomas Jefferson, Proposal Virginia Constitution, *T. Jefferson Papers.* C. J. Boyd, Ed., 1950, 1:334.)

"A militia, when properly formed, are in fact the people themselves... and include all men capable of bearing arms." (Attributed to Richard Henry Lee, *Additional Letters from the Federal Farmer*, 1788, 169.)

"Besides the advantage of being armed, which the Americans possess over the people of almost every other nation, the existence of subordinate governments, to which the people are attached, and by which the militia officers are appointed, forms a barrier against the enterprises of ambition, more insurmountable than any which a simple government of any form can admit of. Notwithstanding the military establishments in the several kingdoms of Europe, which are carried as far as the public resources will bear, the governments are afraid to trust the people with arms." (James Madison, *The Federalist,* Number 46.)

"Before a standing army can rule, the people must be disarmed; as they are in almost every kingdom of Europe. The supreme power in America cannot enforce unjust laws by the sword; because the whole body of the people are armed, and constitute a force superior to any bands of regular troops that can be, on any pretense, raised in the United States." (Noah Webster in "An Examination into the Leading Principles of the Federal Constitution," 1787, a pamphlet aimed at swaying Pennsylvania toward ratification, in Paul Ford, Ed., *Pamphlets on the Constitution of the United States*, New York, 1988, 56.)

"...but if circumstances should at any time oblige the government to form an army of any magnitude, that army can never be formidable to the liberties of the people, while there is a large body of citizens, little if at all inferior to them in discipline and use of arms, who stand ready to defend their rights...." (Alexander Hamilton regarding standing armies, *The Federalist Papers*, Number 29.)

"[The] Constitution [shall] never be construed to authorize Congress to infringe the just liberty of the press or the rights of conscience; or prevent the people of the United States who are peaceable citizens from keeping their own arms." (*Debates and Proceedings in the Convention of the Commonwealth of Massachusetts Held in the Year 1788, and which Finally Ratified the Constitution of the United States.* Boston: William White Printer to the Commonwealth, 1856, 86.)

"The project of disciplining all the militia of the United States is as futile as it would be injurious.... Little more can reasonably be aimed at, with respect to the people at large, than to have them properly armed and equipped." (Alexander Hamilton, *The Federalist Papers,* Number 29.)

"& what country can preserve its liberties, if its rulers are not warned from time to time that their people preserve the spirit of resistance? Let them take arms.... [T]he tree of liberty must be refreshed from time to time with the blood of patriots and tyrants." (Thomas Jefferson in a letter to William S. Smith in Paris, November 13, 1787. *Thomas Jefferson on Democracy,* Saul K. Padover, Ed. New York: New American Library, 1959; see also Library of Congress, www.loc.gov/exhibits/jefferson/105.html.)

"Guard with jealous attention the public liberty. Suspect everyone who approaches that jewel. Unfortunately, nothing will preserve it but downright force. Whenever you give up that force, you are inevitably ruined." (Patrick Henry, in *Debates in the Several State Conventions 3,* 2d ed., Jonathan Elliot, Ed. Philadelphia: Printed for the Editor, 1836, 45.)

"The strongest reason for people to retain the right to keep and bear arms is, as a last resort, to protect themselves against tyranny in government." (Attributed to Thomas Jefferson, *United States of America, Congressional Record, Proceedings and Debates of the 106th Congress,* Second Session, Senate, February 7, 2000, 657.)

"A strong body makes the mind strong.... As to the species of exercises, I advise the gun. While this gives moderate exercise to the body, it gives boldness, enterprise, and independence to the mind. Games played with the ball and others of that nature, are too violent for the body and stamp no character on the mind. Let your gun therefore be the constant companion of your walks." (Thomas Jefferson, in *The Jeffersonian Cyclopedia: A Comprehensive Collection of the Views of Thomas Jefferson,* John P. Foley, Ed. New York: Funk & Wagnalls Company, 1900, 318.)

"What country can preserve its liberties if their rulers are not warned from time to time that their people preserve the spirit of resistance. Let them take arms." (Thomas Jefferson to James Madison, Dec. 20, 1787, in *Papers of Jefferson,* ed. Boyd et al.)

"To trust arms in the hands of the people at large has, in Europe, been believed...to be an experiment fraught only with danger. Here by a long trial it has been proved to be perfectly harmless.... If the government be equitable; if it be reasonable in its exactions; if proper attention be paid to the education of children in knowledge and religion, few men will be disposed to use arms, unless for their amusement, and for the defence of themselves and their country." (Timothy Dwight, *Travels in New England and New York.* New Haven: Timothy Dwight, 1821, 17.)

"The right of the citizens to keep and bear arms has justly been considered as the palladium of the liberties of a republic; since it offers a strong moral check against the usurpation and arbitrary power of rulers; and will generally, even if these are successful in the first instance, enable the people to resist and triumph over them." (Joseph Story, *Commentaries on the Constitution of the United States; With a Preliminary Review of the Constitutional History of the Colonies and States before the Adoption of the Constitution,* Volume II. (Boston: Little and Brown, 1851, 607.)

"The tank, the B-52, the fighter-bomber, the state-controlled police and military are the weapons of dictatorship. The rifle is the weapon of democracy. If guns are outlawed, only the government will have guns. Only the police, the secret police, the military. The hired servants of our rulers. Only the government – and a few outlaws. I intend to be among the outlaws." (Edward Abbey, "The Right to Arms," *Abbey's Road.* New York, Plume, 1979, 130–132.)

"To prohibit a citizen from wearing or carrying a war arm . . . is an unwarranted restriction upon the constitutional right to keep and bear arms. If cowardly and dishonorable men sometimes shoot unarmed men with army pistols or guns, the evil must be prevented by the penitentiary and gallows, and not by a general deprivation of constitutional privilege." (*Wilson v. State,* 33 Ark. 557, at 560, 34 Am. Rep. 52, at 54, 1878, from www.guncite.com/court/state/33ar557.html.)

Appreciation to William J. Federer (Amerisearch.net, American Minute).

A Word from the Publisher

Train up a child in the way he should go, and when he is old he will not depart from it. (Proverbs 22:6[*])

But if anyone does not provide [safety, etc.] for his own [family], and especially for those of his household, he has denied the faith and is worse than an unbeliever. (1 Timothy 5:8[*])

To preserve liberty, it is essential that the whole body of people always possess arms, and be taught alike, especially when young, how to use them. (Richard Henry Lee [1])

The great object is that every man be armed . . . and everyone who is able may have a gun. (Patrick Henry [2])

The right of the people to keep and bear arms shall not be infringed. A well-regulated militia, composed of the body of the people, trained to arms, is the best and most natural defense of a free country. . . . (James Madison [3])

WELCOME to the inaugural children's book in our new series under the imprint "Young Heart Books" – words and pictures for those young folk with tender hearts who are pliable, fun-loving, and eager to learn. Young Heart Books are for children and their parents who want to learn about truth and life. These books are tools to prepare children in the ways of God and His expanding kingdom, to help them grow in the nurture and admonition of the Lord, and to help ready them to serve as a co-regent of Christ by adulthood, as the Lord wills.

This is Kimberly Jo Simac's fourth book for children. It is intended to help motivate and excite youngsters in getting to know their gun as their companion and defender, so that at the proper age they might become confident with their rifle by their side. This book will encourage children to learn how to shoot correctly, how to care properly for their gun, and how to rely upon it for enjoyment, food, and protection. This book will also promote study by children about the role of the Colonial Minutemen and of all the soldiers who have defended our country throughout history. Through this book our youth may begin to understand how to help provide safety for their present family and later their own family.

Above all we seek to encourage the young to seek the Lord in prayer, worship in church, and love the liberties provided by the sacrifices of our country's forefathers, so that they may grow into tomorrow's American patriots.

Since it is our right and duty to protect and provide for our household (1 Tim. 5:8), this may lead to a defense of enemies from without – or even from within – our nation; and this is one of the primary goals of the Constitution's Second Amendment established by our Founding Fathers.

In this respect, parents, I draw your attention to the preceding pages where there are numerous quotations concerning the cautions of those wise men who assembled at the Constitutional Convention to establish the world's first Christian Constitutional Republic, adding a Bill of Rights guaranteeing in its second amendment the right to keep and bear arms. Read on and embrace the profound words of America's servant leaders of the past and ponder and reason with them, preparing for your own and your children's future.

Happy Hunting,
Gerald Christian Nordskog
Publisher
Memorial Day, 2010

---

[*] The New King James Version

[1] Richard Henry Lee, 1788, Initiator of the Declaration of Independence and member of the first Senate which passed the Bill of Rights. Paraphrased from Walter Bennett, ed., *Letters from the Federal Farmer to the Republican.* Tuscaloosa: University of Alabama Press, 1978, 21, 22, 124.

[2] Patrick Henry, in the Virginia Convention on the ratification of the U.S. Constitution. *Debates and other Proceedings of the Convention of Virginia* (taken in shorthand by David Robertson of Petersburg), 2d ed. Richmond: Enquirer Press for Ritchie & Worsley and Augustine Davis, 1805, 271, 275.

[3] James Madison, Father of the Constitution, speaking in Congress to amend the Constitution on June 8, 1789. *Annals of Congress*, 1st Congress, 1st Session, June 8, 1789, 451.

About the Author

Kimberly Jo Simac is a Christian wife, mother, grandmother, and patriotic American. She, together with her husband Butch, has raised nine children in the beautiful Northwoods of Wisconsin. Kim and Butch consider themselves blessed to have nurtured their family in this magnificent country. Kim is thankful to God for being an American. She testifies that it is the blessings of American liberty that have allowed her to experience *the American Dream*.

"I have lived the American Dream and it is my responsibility to assure that under my watch the same potential is left for those who follow. It is a gift that must be guarded, preserved, and passed on."

Simac is a Conservative Activist, a Christian Patriotic Speaker, and has a Conservative Radio Talk Show.

She is a favorite speaker; her message of American Exceptionalism is always well received. At her appearances, Simac is devoted to teaching American children to have pride in this great country. This noble commitment, along with her grassroots work in her hometown, has established her as a leader in the battle to save American values and principles.

When not working on children's books or her other enterprises, Kim and Butch raise Warmblood sport horses at their Eagle River training facility, where Kim coaches future equestrian stars.

Kim hopes her children's books will encourage youth to have high aspirations and to be proud of who they are. She anticipates that her books will teach honor for God our Father and ignite the spark of patriotism that is in every child's heart.

About the Artist

Donna Goeddaeus lives in the middle of a vast forest alongside a river in northern Wisconsin. She is a self-taught award-winning artist who enjoys painting on commission, teaching fine art, and illustrating children's books.

"I was thrilled when Kim asked me to illustrate this book," she said. "I love our country deeply and feel strongly about the protection of our God-given freedoms passed down to us by our Founding Fathers and defended by all the men and women over the years who have given so much. It is an honor to illustrate such an important message for our nation's children."

When she is not busy illustrating, Donna hikes with her dogs, canoes and fishes the river, and goes on long trail rides with her horse, Cochise. "It's a great life," she adds. "Art, nature, and my faith in God are the best things in my life."

Twelve books presented by Nordskog Publishing
Meaty, tasty, and easily digestible Biblical treasures!

The Fear of God: A Forgotten Doctrine
by Arnold L. Frank, DMin

Gives the reader both a godly rebuke and an impassioned plea to hear the Word of God and the wise counsel of the Puritans speak about the fear of God, which precedes the love of God. **EXPANDED 2ND EDITION** includes Scripture Index and Study Questions.

ISBN 978-0-9796736-5-8 **PB** 6"x9" 228 PP
2008 **$16.95**

Died He for Me: A Physician's View of the Crucifixion of Jesus Christ
by Mark A. Marinella, MD, FACP

"The death of Jesus for our sins is the heart of the Christian faith. What does a physician have to say about that death? In this important new book, particularly intriguing are the details of the death of Jesus as found in the Old Testament, written hundreds of years before."
— Jerry Newcombe, DMin

SPANISH EDITION— Por Mí, El Murio
2009 **$14.95**

ISBN 978-0-9796736-6-5
PB 6"x9" 144 PP 2008
$13.95

Truth Standing on Its Head: Insight for an Extraordinary Christian Walk from The Sermon on the Mount by John N. Day, PhD

Dr. John Day, Bible scholar and pastor, begins with the paradoxical Beatitudes and takes us through our Lord's greatest Sermon in depth, offering readers a "mind-expanding and life-transforming" experience. How can the meek inherit the earth? How are the persecuted blessed? While these are not things that we naturally associate with happiness, this is Jesus' startling opposite-from-the-world way of bringing us into the most blessed and happy life —an extraordinary christian walk. ISBN978-0-9824929-3-2
HB-CASEBOUND 6"x9" 192PP 2010 **$18.95**

God's Ten Commandments: Yesterday, Tod Forever by Francis Nigel Lee, LLB, DJur, DCL, PhI

"God gave man Ten Commandments. Every one of the vital, in all ages. God Himself is the Root of the Moral and perfectly reflects it. It is the very basis of the U States and every other Common Law nation in the w
—Dr. Francis Nigel Lee

"Dr. Lee is a man deeply devoted to God. I am happy to commend to your reading Dr. Lee's work."
—The Honorable Roy S. Moore
former Chief Justice, Alabama Supreme Court, and President of the Foundation for Moral Law, Inc.

ISBN 978-0-9796736-2-7
5"x8" 128 PP
EXTENSIVE APPENDIX INCLUDING GOD'S ETERNAL MORAL LAW CHART
PB 2007 **$11.95**

Loving God with All Your Heart: Keeping the Greatest Commandment in Everyday Life
by Susie Hobson

This small book offers a huge practical encouragement for grounding yourself in the Bible and developing a deep personal relationship with God as the firm foundation for living and serving and experiencing ultimate and unfailing love. You will love Susie's personal testimony.

ISBN 978-0-9824929-6-3 **HB**-CASEBOUND 5"x 8" 116 PP
2010 **$15.95**

A Whole New World: The Gospel According to Revelation by Greg Uttinger

"**Greg Uttinger**'s book is refreshing for its brevity; it does not confuse the reader in the minutia of exposition. It de-mystifies Revelation by focusing the reader on the big picture. I encourage anyone to read it. The blessing on those who read, hear, and keep the message of Revelation (1:3) was referring to its core message—that we serve the risen, victorious Lord of time and eternity. Uttinger's book is faithful to that 'Revelation of Jesus Christ' (1:1)." —Mark R. Rushdoony, President, Chalcedon Foundation

"The author clearly and simply puts forth a very realistic interpretation, taken from Scripture as a whole. He deciphers symbolism from the Word of God and concisely explains the glorious future all believers cherish in anticipation of God's ordained 'Whole New World'." —Gerald Christian Nordskog, Publisher

ISBN 978-0-9796736-0-3 **PB** 5"x 8" 100 PP
2007 **$9.95**

Nourishment from the Word: Select Studie Reformed Doctrine by Kenneth L. Gentry, Jr

This book is a welcomed collection of shorter writings for se Christians following the Biblical encouragement to "be a good se of Jesus Christ, constantly nourished on the words of faith a sound doctrine" (1 Tim. 4:6). **Dr. Kenneth L. Gentry, Jr.** provides a banquet of nourishing entrees too seldom found on the menu of the modern church, to help hungry believers grow in understanding.

Dr. Gentry's deep study of Holy Writ, and his precise and gentle, loving style of communicating, make this book a must for pastors and laypersons alike who want to follow Jesus lovingly, obediently, and wisely. We need to consume the meat and not just the milk of theology. Wisdom is the principle thing, so says the Word of God. Come, eat, and be satisfied.

ISBN 978-0-9796736-4-1 **PB** 6"x9" 188 PP
2008 **$15.95**

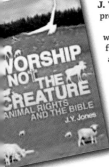